Dear Parent:
Your child's love of reading starts here!

Every child learns to read in a different way and at his or her own speed. Some go back and forth between reading levels and read favorite books again and again. Others read through each level in order. You can help your young reader improve and become more confident by encouraging his or her own interests and abilities. From books your child reads with you to the first books he or she reads alone, there are I Can Read Books for every stage of reading:

SHARED READING
Basic language, word repetition, and whimsical illustrations, ideal for sharing with your emergent reader

BEGINNING READING
Short sentences, familiar words, and simple concepts for children eager to read on their own

READING WITH HELP
Engaging stories, longer sentences, and language play for developing readers

READING ALONE
Complex plots, challenging vocabulary, and high-interest topics for the independent reader

I Can Read Books have introduced children to the joy of reading since 1957. Featuring award-winning authors and illustrators and a fabulous cast of beloved characters, I Can Read Books set the standard for beginning readers.

A lifetime of discovery begins with the magical words **"I Can Read!"**

Visit www.icanread.com for information
on enriching your child's reading experience.

I Can Read® and I Can Read Book® are trademarks of HarperCollins Publishers.

Pete the Cat's Family Road Trip
Text copyright © 2020 by Kimberly and James Dean
Art copyright © 2020 by James Dean
Pete the Cat is a registered trademark of Pete the Cat, LLC.
www.icanread.com
Library of Congress Control Number: 2019944600
ISBN 978-0-06-286839-8 (trade bdg.) — ISBN 978-0-06-286838-1 (pbk.)
Book design by Chrisila Maida

19 20 21 22 23 SCP 10 9 8 7 6 5 4 3 2 1 ❖ First Edition

I Can Read!

BEGINNING 1 READING

Pete the Cat's
FAMILY ROAD TRIP

by Kimberly & James Dean

HARPER

An Imprint of HarperCollinsPublishers

Pete, Bob, Mom, and Dad
are going on a road trip
across the United States!

Dad loads the bags onto the roof.

Mom picks the music.

Bob and Pete grab the bike.

The first stop is Niagara Falls.

They ride a boat

to see the waterfall up close.

Pete loves pretending he's the captain.

Next stop is Boston!

The family walks the Freedom Trail.

They take a photo

in front of Paul Revere's house.

"Historic and cool," says Bob.

Now they are off to a new city.

It is New York City!

The family takes an elevator
to the top of One World Trade Center.
"Look, it's the Statue of Liberty,"
says Dad.

In Savannah, they ride a riverboat.

Pete orders a slice of peach pie.

"Yum," says Pete.

"Life is good."

When they arrive at Key West,

Pete meets a six-toed cat.

"Your paws are groovy," says Pete.

"Right back at you," says the cat.

New Orleans is famous

for jazz music.

The groovy jazz music makes
everyone dance in the streets!

Everyone is excited about the next stop.

But then . . . uh-oh!

The car gets a flat tire on Route 66.

"Don't worry," says Mom.

"We can't let this ruin our trip!"

Mom and Dad change the tire.

Soon the family is on their way again!

19

Mom parks the car.

"Look over there," says Bob.

It's Mount Rushmore.

What a sight to see!

The family stops to take a photo.

At Yellowstone National Park,
everyone unwinds.

The park is so pretty and peaceful.

Bob sees bison snacking on grass.

"Check out those horns," says Mom.

Suddenly, Old Faithful shoots water

high into the air.

"Cool," says Pete.

Bob thinks it's time to try something different than a car ride.

The family goes on a horse ride instead
in Utah's Monument Valley!

In Los Angeles, Pete checks out
the Cat Hollywood Walk of Fame.

Pete puts his paws in the pawprints.

"I feel like a star," he says.

When they get to San Francisco,
they all squeeze into a cable car.

Pete stands in the front and says,
"Toot toot!"

The last stop is Seattle.

They go to the top of the Space Needle.

"Wow," says Mom.

"This city is pretty at night."

Finally it is time to go home.

"We saw so many cool places,"
says Bob.

"What was your favorite part
of the road trip?" asks Mom.

Pete thinks long and hard.

There were so many neat sights.

"The best part was being together
with you all," says Pete.